HOME AT LAST

RASCHKA & WILLIAMS

GREENWILLOW BOOKS

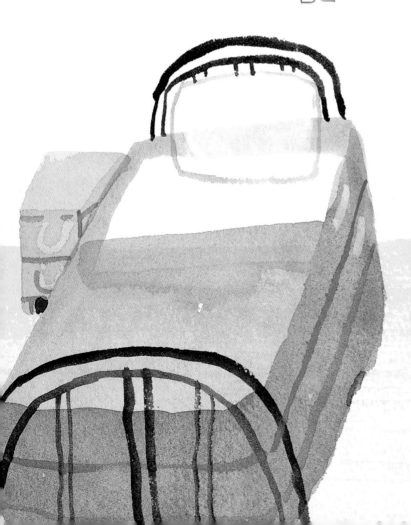
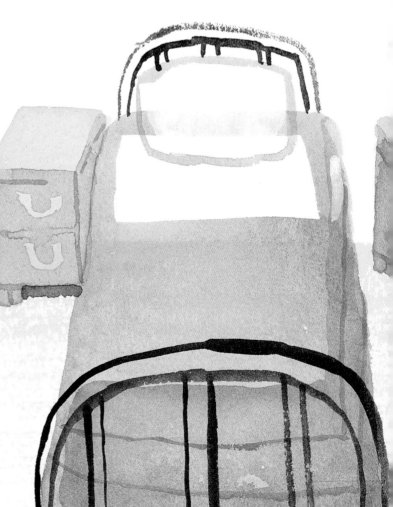

Lester tripped over the laces of his new shoes just as he went out the door and down the steps of the children's center. He was rushing, because he wanted to be outside when his new parents arrived in their car with their dog, Wincka. Daddy Albert and Daddy Rich had finally—at last and really and truly—adopted Lester.

It always takes a long time to adopt someone. Lester had visited Daddy Albert and Daddy Rich a lot. He had a picture by his bed of the three of them, plus Wincka. In the picture they already looked like a family. But it had taken a whole year for the paperwork to be finished.

Lester saw a car coming down the street. "They're here!"

Lester stood in front of the center while Daddy Albert tied his shoelaces into firm double knots.

"All set now," said Daddy Rich, reaching for Lester's hand.

Daddy Albert carried Lester's big suitcase, and Lester held tightly to his little blue suitcase and his favorite yo-yo. He kept turning to check on Wincka, who waddled along behind them. They were going to Daddy Albert and Daddy Rich's car. Lester loved that car. He intended to drive it himself as soon as he could!

When they got to the house, Lester helped his new Daddy Albert and his new Daddy Rich put his new clothes into his new drawers. He slipped his yo-yo into his pocket and followed them to put his big suitcase away with the other suitcases up in the attic. As they climbed the steep stairs, Daddy Rich pretended the attic was a haunted house.

"You won't need this suitcase anymore, sport," Albert told him. "No more moving here and there and everywhere. You're home with us now."

But Lester would not let his little blue suitcase stay up there in the attic. He showed Daddy Rich that it was full of his best action toys.

"Those will look neat lined up in your new toy cupboard," said Daddy Rich.

But the little suitcase was where they had always lived. "They have to stay right here in case anyone comes to hurt me," said Lester.

Lester kept the blue suitcase right beside his bed. Often he set up the action figures all around the floor, with his yo-yo and its string tangled amongst them. Sometimes he forgot and stumbled over them, and Wincka click-clicked on her toenails around them, but it was Albert, his new dad with the great big feet, who tripped the most. When Albert complained, Lester insisted that he needed his action figures and his suitcase right there, where he could reach them easily. "But I'll keep all the guys packed," he promised.

So every evening, after Rich or Albert read him a story and tucked him in and Wincka eased off the foot of the bed to follow them out of the room, Lester talked to his action figures. Afterward, he carefully arranged them in the suitcase and zippered them in. Then he tried a few tricky maneuvers on his yo-yo before putting it under his pillow and shutting his eyes.

ut late every single night, Lester would appear in his parents' room with that suitcase—first in the doorway and then moving silently to the foot of the bed, where he would pat Wincka on her wrinkled velvety forehead. The first few times he made this night trip, Wincka snuffled and barked a little and shifted her great weight a lot. But she was getting older and she loved her sleep. Soon Lester could tiptoe right by her to the head of the bed, and there he would stand, waiting and waiting and waiting and swooping one of his guys over his daddies' sleeping bodies.

When Daddy Rich and Daddy Albert finally opened their very sleepy eyes and saw their new son, Lester, standing by their bed, they would say, "What's wrong? What's the trouble, sport?" Daddy Rich would feel Lester's forehead for fever and ask if he was too cold or too hot or hungry.

A few times Daddy Rich and Daddy Albert, followed by Wincka, even took Lester into the kitchen and fixed him hot cocoa and toast. His daddies sleepily slurped up the cocoa and Wincka sleepily crunched up the toast, because it was not cocoa and toast Lester wanted.

MOMMMMME WHO WILL TAKE CARE OF ME DADDY

What Lester wanted was to climb into his parents' bed, too. More than anything, he longed to wriggle right into the middle of that bed, with Daddy Rich on one side and Daddy Albert on the other side and fat old Wincka at his feet, and to have his action figures in their blue suitcase right on the floor beside them. That way he knew he would be safe from everything bad in the whole world.

Lester never told Daddy Rich and Daddy Albert about this. But every night, as though he had an alarm clock ringing in his belly, he grabbed his suitcase and made his expedition down the hall and through the door to the side of the bed.

To Lester, the middle-of-the-night quiet was the quiet of a strange house. It had a persistent whisper in it, and he was sure that whisper would eventually get Daddy Rich to mutter, "What's up, little guy?" or get Albert to swing his long legs and big feet off the bed and into his great big slippers and to stand up and put his arms around Lester. And never let him go.

Lester's first parents had died in a bad car crash when he was little, and he had lived with his grandma until she became very old and sick. Then he had lived in the children's center with many other children for a long time, before he came to live with just Albert and Rich and Wincka.

"He must think it's really odd to end up with two fathers," said Daddy Albert.

"Well, we are very good fathers," said Daddy Rich.

"But I expect he never imagined us and Wincka when he dreamed of being adopted," Daddy Albert said.

"No, but maybe he imagined elephants!" said Daddy Rich, smiling.

Daddy Rich and Daddy Albert had decided, long before they finished adopting Lester, that it was important for their new little boy to have his own room and his own bed. They had spent many weekends painting the room and finding the right bed for the boy who was coming to live with them. And they surely knew, from living with Wincka, how impossible it was to get a creature out of your bed once you have let that creature in, if only in an emergency . . . if only for a few nights.

So each night, in the middle of the night, Rich or Albert led Lester back to his own bed. They sat with him and talked about the yo-yo contest he was registered for, and baseball and his new cousins and all the things they planned to do together. They asked him about his friends at the center.

They explained that all of them in bed together was special for Sunday mornings. Mornings when they could sleep late and no one had to go to work or school. And perhaps they could even eat pancakes in bed. But only on Sundays and maybe New Year's Day and the Fourth of July.

They explained and explained more times than they had ever expected to explain anything to anyone. Daddy Rich sang Lester every song he knew. Daddy Albert told him every story he could remember.

In the mornings they were always sleepy. Daddy Rich burned their breakfast. Daddy Albert lost the car keys and couldn't find his glasses and was late for work. But none of these things kept Lester from his nightly expedition down the hall and to the side of their big bed.

Daddy Rich brought home a new two-wheeler. It was Lester's first bike ever. Lester was so excited, he learned how to ride it in no time. He loved riding around his new neighborhood with Daddy Rich.

One day, as they licked the last of their cones from the ice cream man's truck, Daddy Rich said, "See, little guy, life's not so bad."

Then Lester wadded up his napkin, and standing on his tiptoes, he reached up and wiped the strawberry ice cream from Daddy Rich's mustache.

"Hey, who's the dad here, little fella, me or you?" Rich asked, grabbing Lester around the middle.

Lester was so happy. He rammed his head into Daddy Rich's belly and the two of them ended up in a sticky, silly wrestling bout—and Lester won!

Daddy Rich was an easygoing kind of father. But Daddy Albert had a big temper. After many nights of Lester's expeditions into his parents' bedroom, Daddy Albert lost that temper. He knocked the action figure out of Lester's hand. He pulled Lester down the hall and back to his own room. "THIS BED IS YOUR BED and THIS IS WHERE YOU MUST SLEEP!" he boomed at Lester.

Lester started to cry. He was suddenly very, very frightened by the angry screaming face of his new Daddy Albert.

But just as quickly as Daddy Albert had turned into the maddest face of Lester's imagining, he turned back into a good Daddy Albert. His booming voice softened. He hugged Lester close. "What, what is it?" he said. "Try to tell me."

"It's lonely in here with just me," Lester said, squeezing out the words. "There's all three of you in your bed in there, and in here is nobody. Just me. Just me. I'm scared. What if somebody comes and takes me away right in the middle of the night? What if bad people come really quiet on tiptoes, or what if they fly in and you don't even hear them?"

Daddy Albert felt so sad. He rocked Lester and listened to his sobs and worried.

Daddy Rich listened, and tickled Lester's back, and worried, too.

But Wincka listened, and Wincka took action.

Wincka rose majestically from the foot of the big bed and padded into Lester's room. She jumped up on Lester's bed and arranged herself at the end of it. She closed her eyes and huffed a sigh and went right back to sleep, as if to say, All settled. She didn't even snuffle when Lester switched around the covers and himself, so that Wincka at the foot of the bed could become his pillow. She didn't even stir when Lester fell fast asleep with his head on her warm back.

Daddy Albert wiped Lester's nose with a tissue. He carefully lifted a tear from Lester's eyelash. "Now I bet you'll sleep," he whispered.

He showed the tear to Daddy Rich and that made Daddy Rich cry a few tears of his own.

Then both Daddy Albert and Daddy Rich kissed Lester good-night, and they kissed Wincka, too.

"Lester is a great kid, a brave kid," said Daddy Rich. "Once he makes some new friends, he'll be out on a skateboard and playing ball and sleeping through the night. You'll see."

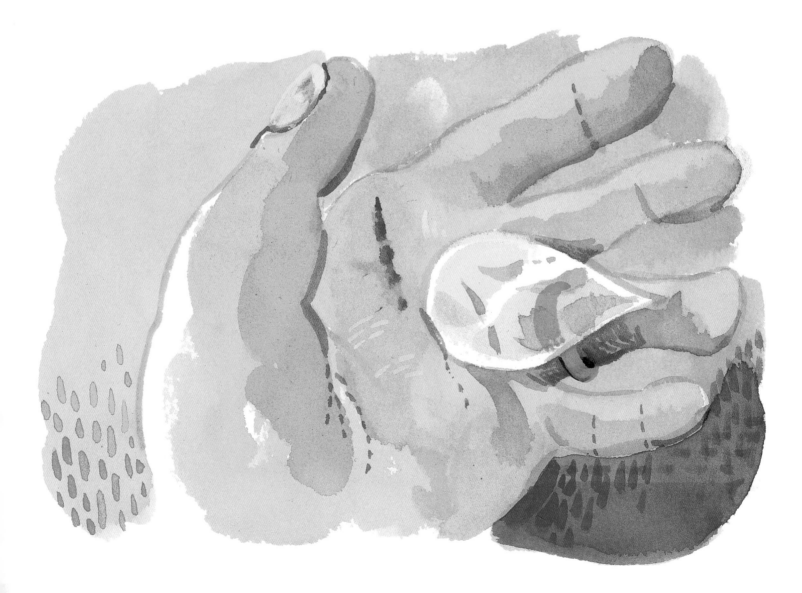

Daddy Albert remembered it was not so easy to make friends in a new place. The kids think you're a different species, like from Mars.

Both daddies took one long fond look at their son. "Lester will make it just fine, and he's still got his defender guys," said Albert. "He'll depend on them less and less, now that he's got you and me on his side."

"And Wincka, too," Rich added.

"Two not-so-smart dads. One brilliant dog," said Albert. "Maybe Wincka should have adopted Lester instead of us."

And that's exactly what Wincka did. She decided that Lester and Lester's bed belonged to her, too. And though Daddy Rich sometimes woke up missing the weight of Wincka on his feet—because they had been sleeping that way for such a long time—that was okay with him.

On Sunday mornings, Wincka would return to her time-honored spot at the foot of the big bed. Room was made for Lester in the middle of the big bed. And soon, Silver, a big old cat who used to belong to Rich's mother (now Lester's new grandma), came to live with them, too. She liked to curl up right by Daddy Rich. That bed was crowded! Pancakes and toast crumbs and Sunday papers and slanty shadows and sunlit stripes from the window blinds were all in and on the bed.

That was what Lester loved best about his new life, those Sunday mornings.

But he also loved when his new cousins—all four of them—stayed over on Saturday nights. They laughed and jumped around and played and played so much that they hardly slept a wink.

And at first light, they piled right on top of Daddy Rich and Daddy Albert.

"Help! We're being attacked!" the daddies shouted, dashing through the house chased by cousins and Lester and Wincka and even Silver. And then it was pancakes for everyone. And then an entire day of more games and walks and snacks and fun together.

Lester was truly home at last.

To my lucky stars—V. B. W.

For Vera—C. R.

Vera B. Williams wished to thank and acknowledge Claudine Luchsinger for her invaluable organizational assistance and research skills and her generous and positive spirit; and Sylvie Le Floc'h, Virginia Duncan, and Chris Raschka for traveling to Narrowsburg to work so intently, quickly, and happily with her to complete the book.

Watercolor paints on paper were used to prepare the full-color art. The text type is Carre Noir Pro.

Library of Congress Cataloging-in-Publication Data is available.
ISBN 978-0-06-134973-7 (trade ed.)—ISBN 978-0-06-134974-4 (lib. bdg.)
"Greenwillow Books."
16 17 18 19 20 SCP 10 9 8 7 6 5 4 3 2 1
First Edition

Greenwillow Books

Vera B. Williams wrote *Home at Last* and then put it aside for many years in order to focus on other work, family, and life. In the spring of 2015, she decided that the time was right and that this beautiful, honest, and personal story needed to be told. Uncertain that she would have the energy to complete the pictures, she invited her good friend Chris Raschka to collaborate with her on what would be her final book. Chris and Vera spent many hours drawing together and planning the design, layout, and pagination of the book. Vera had completed the black-and-white sketches, and seen and loved a sample color picture or two, before she died peacefully at her home in Narrowsburg, New York, on October 16, 2015.

In the summer, Vera called me and said, "Chris, I need help with my book. Can you do it?" I said I could do it. "One more thing," said Vera. "Can you draw action figures?"

Pretty soon I was sitting next to Vera at her kitchen table (which is a lot like my kitchen table), where we read her story and talked. Vera said, "It might be nice if Lester was looking sad right here." I drew what that might look like on a little piece of paper and stuck it down. Vera said, "Here is where Wincka gets her big idea!" And I drew Wincka, the dog, very small and sketchy, and stuck it down where it might go. And so on.

Over the next few months we sat—sometimes together, sometimes apart—and drew. And we talked as we drew.

Vera said, "Daddy Rich is the sporty one. Daddy Albert is a little more nervous. He gets cranky. Lester is really me." She said, "Let's just put out next to us whatever colors we have and then grab them, and when a color runs out just grab another one." We sat together on her sun porch and drew until the sun sank down.

One morning when I arrived, Vera sat in the middle of a pile of fresh drawings. "I don't sleep much anymore," she said, with a great smile. "And I had an explosion of ideas! I've been thinking about the action figures."

The first time we sat together, Vera said, "It's exciting making a book. It's what keeps you alive." She smiled and winked without closing an eye.

Vera no longer sits next to me. Nevertheless, I hear her voice.
This is the book Vera and I made together.
Vera wrote it. Vera and I drew it. And I painted it.